THE NEWSPAPER ANTI COLORING BOOK®

Weather
Sunny and beautiful

For Those Who Are Young at Art

Susan Striker

The Only Newspaper You Write Yourself

AN OWL BOOK
Henry Holt and Company New York

Today is: **Month:** **Day:** **Year:**

TODAY'S BIG NEWS:

A photo taken at the scene.

Picture credit

Published by Henry Holt and Company, Inc., 115 West 18th Street, New York, New York 10011.
Published in Canada by Fitzhenry & Whiteside Limited, 91 Granton Drive, Richmond Hill, Ontario L4B 2N5.

ISBN 0-8050-1599-X (An Owl Book: pbk.)

Henry Holt books are available at special discounts for bulk purchases for sales promotions, premiums, fund-raising, or educational use. Special editions or book excerpts can also be created to specification.

For details contact: Special Sales Director, Henry Holt and Company, Inc., 115 West 18th Street, New York, New York 10011.

First Edition—1992

DESIGNED BY PAULA R. SZAFRANSKI
Printed in the United States of America
Recognizing the importance of preserving the written word, Henry Holt and Company, Inc., by policy, prints all of its first editions on acid-free paper. ∞
10 9 8 7 6 5 4 3 2 1

To Jason with love,
and with gratitude and love to Bob

TODAY'S QUOTE

"It is better to be making the news than taking it; to be an actor rather than a critic."

—*Sir Winston Churchill*

The Anti-Coloring Books®
Founded in 1978
Publisher: Henry Holt and Company
Author: Susan Striker
Editor: Jo Ann Haun
Super Agent: Christine Tomasino
Art Department:
Susan Striker
Sally Schaedler
with
Jason Striker
George Love
Joe Dyas
Maggie MacGowan
Brent Brolin
David Vozar
Katie Cargiulo
Judy Francis
Peter Popiearski

CONTENTS

EDITORIAL

"What's new?" The question is on everyone's lips. Many of us start the day reading the morning newspaper and end it reading the "final" or watching the late-night newscast. The news is both wonderful and terrible. We read of births and deaths, marriages and murders, friendships and fighting. We laugh at the comics and cry over life's tragedies. It can be fun to read about how the rich shop and party, and sobering to ponder the problems of the poor. But it can be fun to write the news, too. Newspapers employ reporters, editors, artists, and photographers. Imagine a job that pays you to go to and write about your favorite event, be it a movie, play, art exhibit, sports event, fashion show, or restaurant opening. Boundless curiosity is the most important qualification.

And, of course, it isn't just other people who make the news. Our own births, marriages, and deaths are likely to be recorded for others to read about. What else would we want to share with the world? Will it be good or bad? Will we rob a bank or write a symphony? Deface a building with spray paint or create a masterpiece that will hang in a museum? All of us share the same joys and disappointments. We don't just read the news, we make it.

EXTRA! EXTRA!
THE NEWSPAPER
ANTI
COLORING BOOK®
GOOD NEWS
Picture credit

EXTRA! EXTRA!
THE NEWSPAPER
ANTI
COLORING BOOK®
BAD NEWS
NEWSTAND

Amazing Rescue

Monkeys Found

Two monkeys who disappeared from the zoo yesterday were discovered playing happily

ARCHAEOLOGISTS DISCOVER ARTIFACT

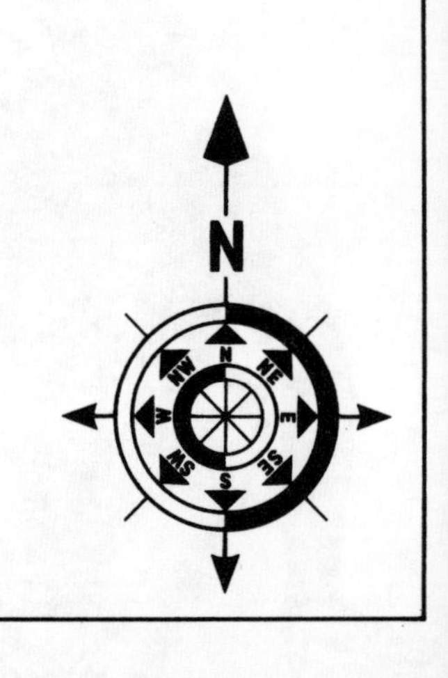

Map of Archaeological Site

LEADER OF DIG REPORTS ON SIGNIFICANCE OF DISCOVERY

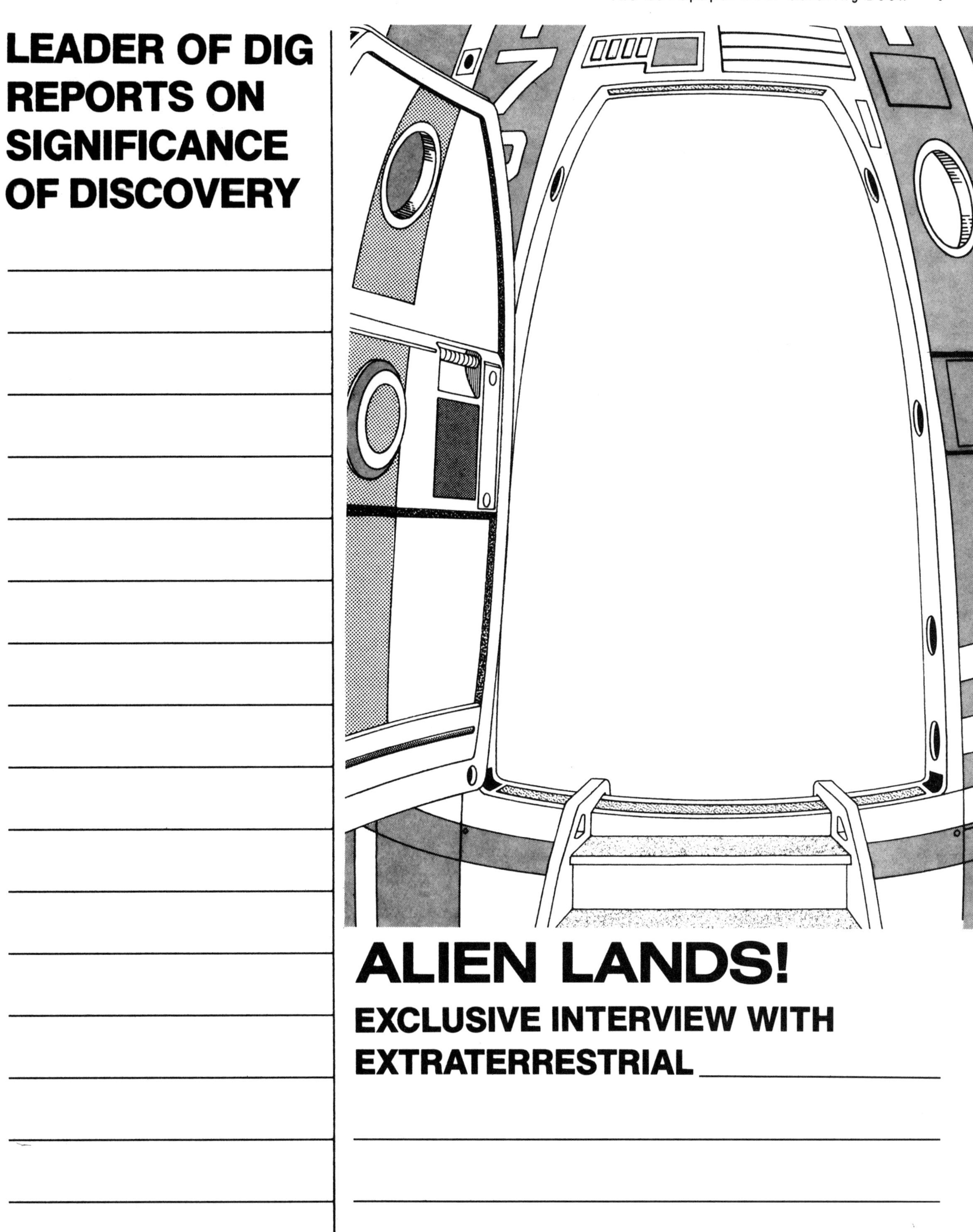

ALIEN LANDS!

EXCLUSIVE INTERVIEW WITH EXTRATERRESTRIAL

IMAGINATIVE FLOATS MAKE

HOLIDAY PARADE A SUCCESS

News of the Nation

USA
29
SPECIAL
FIRST CLASS
Dear Editor,
FIRST CLASS
Address your letters to: The Anti-Coloring Books, c/o Henry Holt and Company, Inc.,
115 West 18th Street, New York, New York 10011.

INTERNATIONAL NEWS

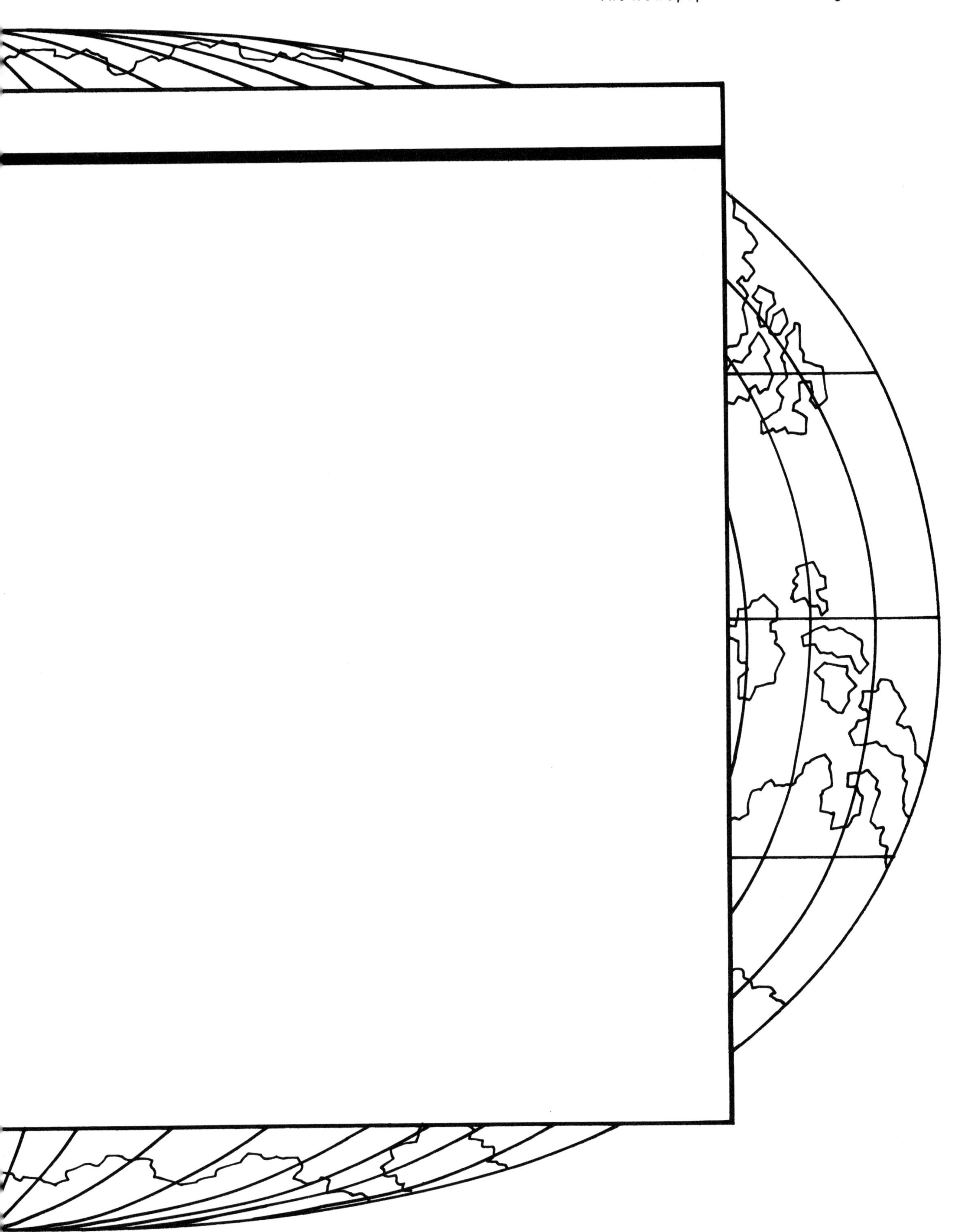

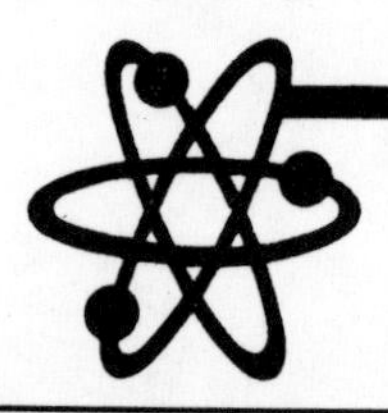

SCIENCE NEWS

New Planet Discovered Between Neptune and Pluto

You have sighted it first and been given the honor of naming it. The new planet will be called ______________________________

Scientists Create New Species

Weather News

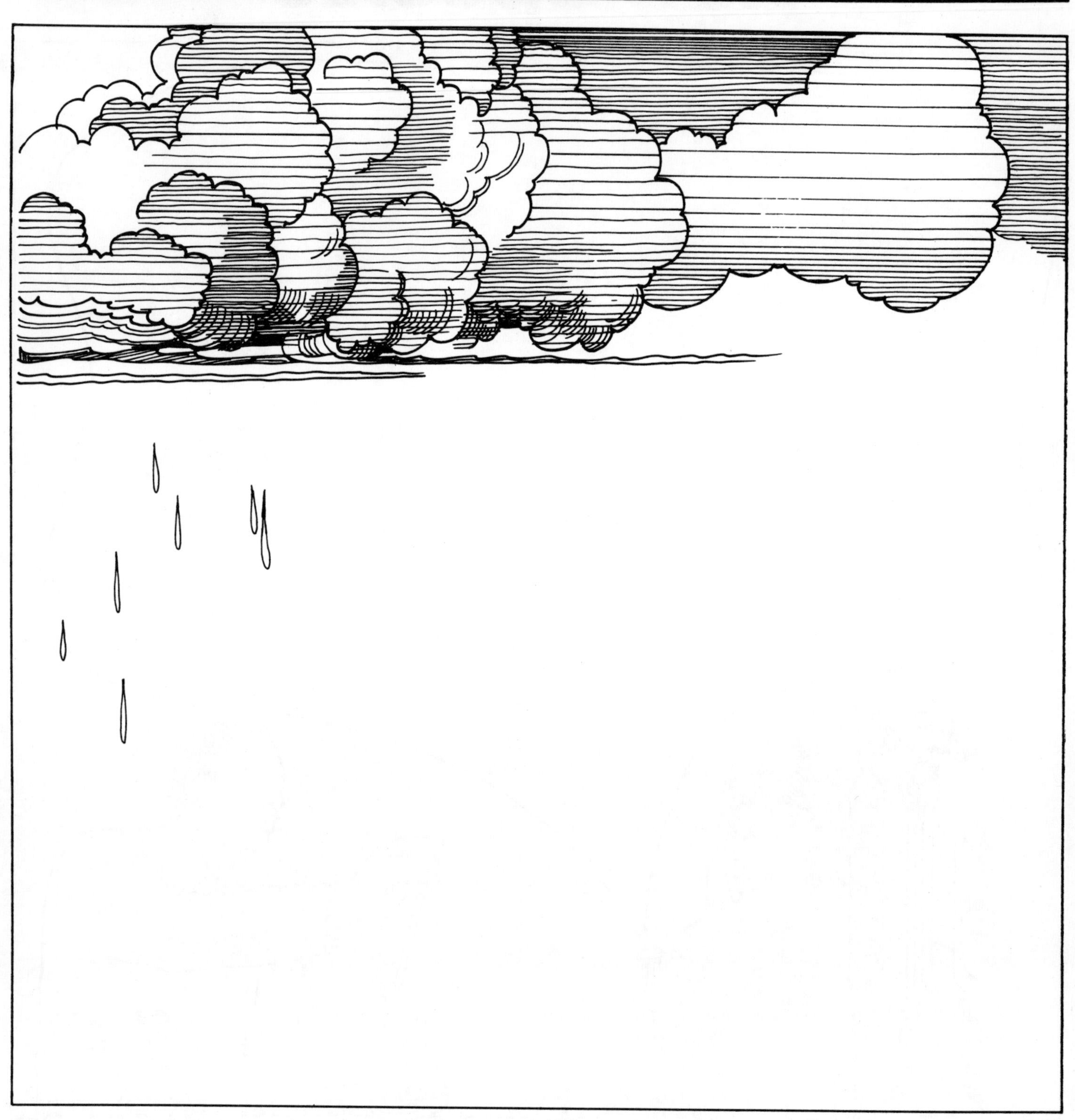

Heavy rains give people a chance to enjoy their favorite rainy-day activities.

Snowstorm up north inspires a snowperson-building contest.

Children down south are making the best of a long heat wave.

Creative Window Displays

Designers were challenged to create window displays interesting enough to compete with the futuristic design of this store.

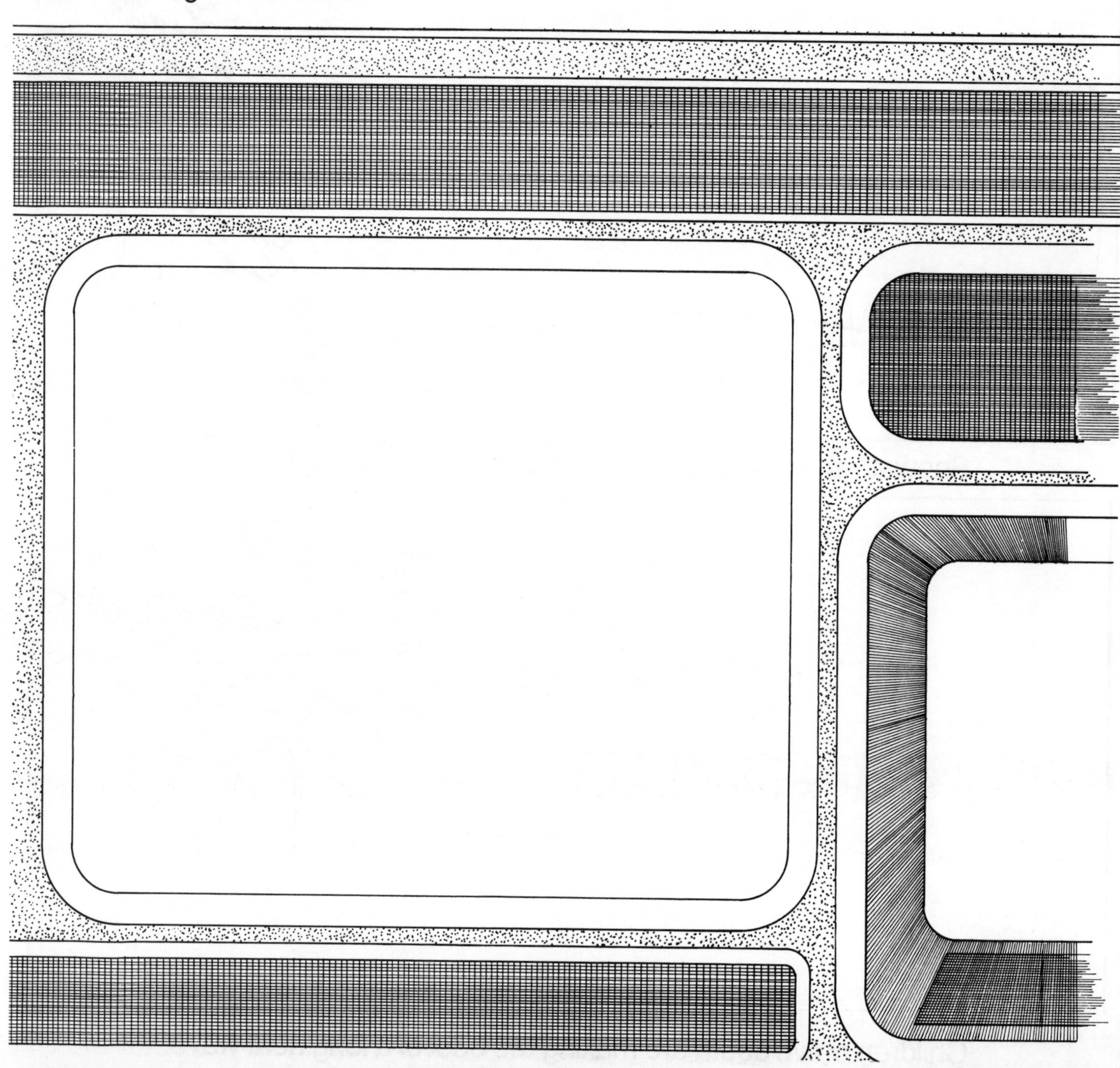

PROMISING NEW INVENTION!

Washington, D.C.—The U.S. Patent Office recently disclosed news of an application to patent a new invention. The innovative new product is expected to have a significant impact on our daily lives. Here's an exclusive look at the patent application.

United States of America Patent Office
Washington, D.C.
Official Application for Patent

File # ____________

Inventor: ____________

Please describe your invention. Include information about how it works and what its advantages are.

____

____

____

Please provide a sketch of your invention.

Exciting New Business Idea

A student has a brilliant idea for a new business. The young entrepreneur describes it in an exclusive interview.

Help Wanted

Imagine yourself at the perfect job. Write the ad that convinced you to apply.

Pet News

The judges saw many fine pets before choosing their favorite.

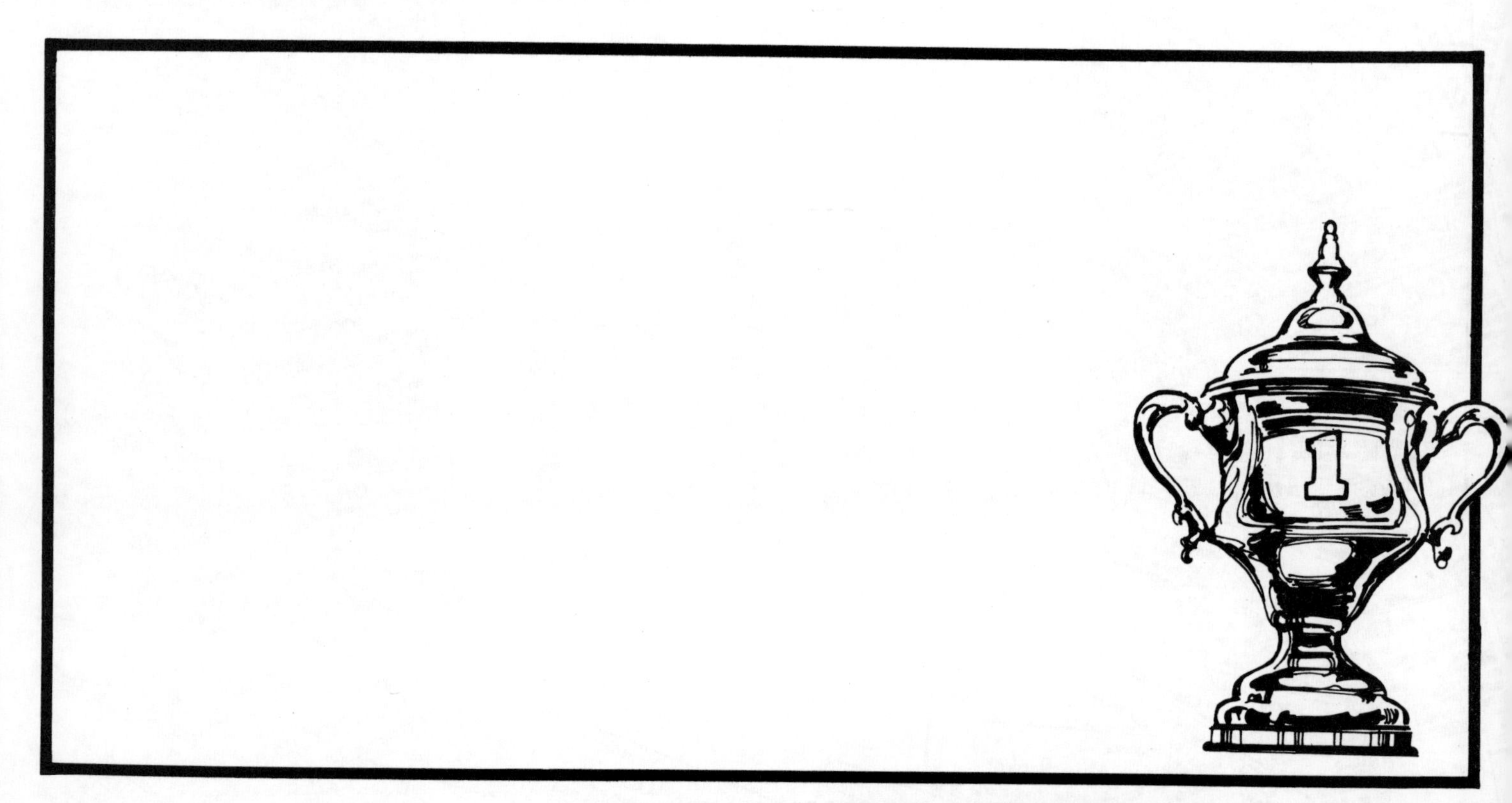

THE WINNER!

You are a world-famous author. The story you wrote about why your pet is important to you has been printed in today's paper.

SCHOOL NEWS

NEW PLAYGROUND DESIGN IS SEEN FOR THE FIRST TIME

From the playground designer:

"My primary concerns in designing the new playground were

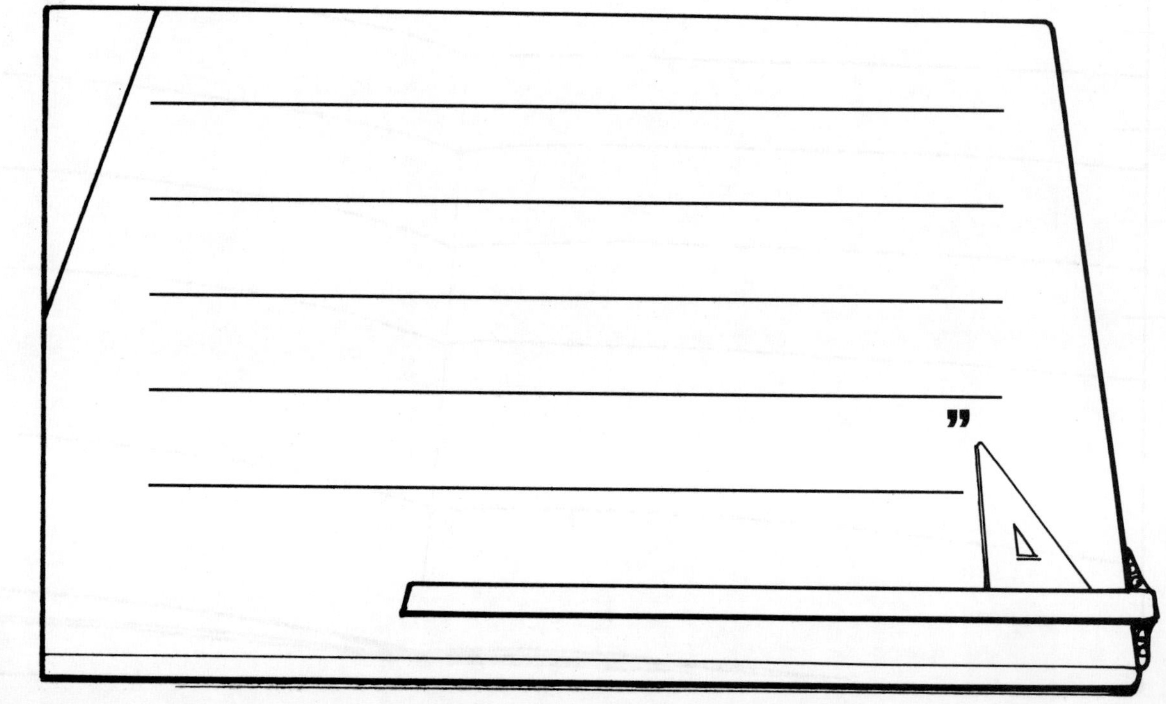

Last Year's "Most Promising Student" Wrote About the First Year on His Own

VALEDICTORIAN GIVES INSPIRATIONAL SPEECH TO CLASSMATES

This is what the outstanding pupil had to say:

THE SCHOOL PLAY WAS A SMASH HIT!

THE MOST EXCITING SPORTS EVENT OF THE SCHOOL YEAR

People are talking about...

Wedding Announcements

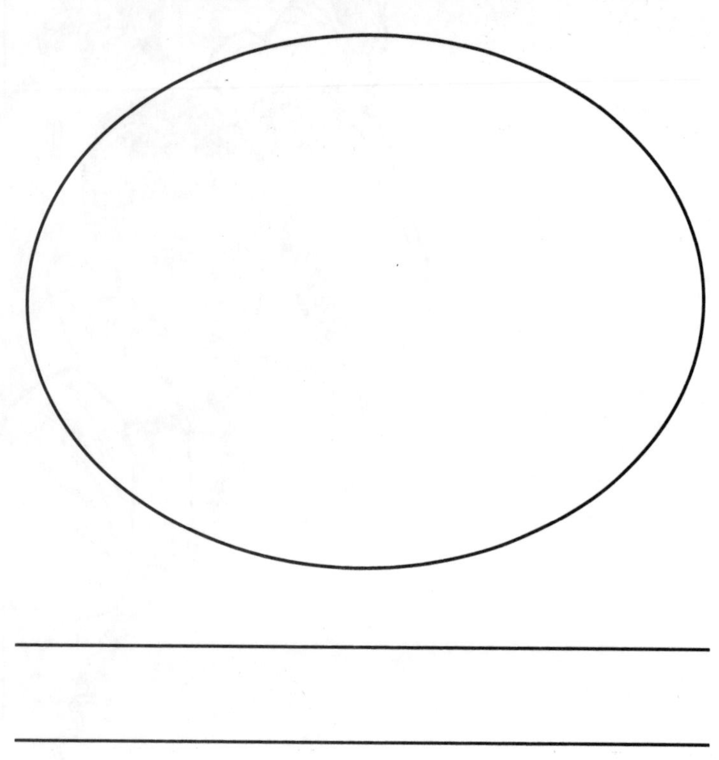

The perfect gift!
Obituary
Think about how you will live your life and what people will say about you after you die. Write your own obituary.

Dear Ms. Advice

Ms. Advice

Dear ms, Advice
What can I do to make the girls like me.?
Sincerely, Fred

Dear Ms. Advice,
What can I do to make the boys like me?
Suzy Q

ARTS & ENTERTAINMENT

A scene from the party everyone is talking about

Here's why... ______________________________

____

____

____

____

____

NIGHTLIFE

ELEGANT NEW NIGHTCLUB ATTRACTS THE ATTENTION OF THE PAPARAZZI

Fashion Highlights

Art News

Famous Portraitist Comes to Town to Paint Your Portrait

Tranquil country scene inspires landscape artist

Cityscape inspires urban artist

Open-air art exhibit draws large crowd of art lovers

Travel News

Your dream vacation

Fabulous ski house for rent

You are the book reviewer. Review the best book you have ever read.

Book Review

Can you really judge a book by its cover? This is the cover of the worst book you ever read.

Design a cover that will encourage others to buy your favorite book.

Theater News
Artists design billboard that will advertise the play of the year

Theatergoers Enjoy the Big Hit

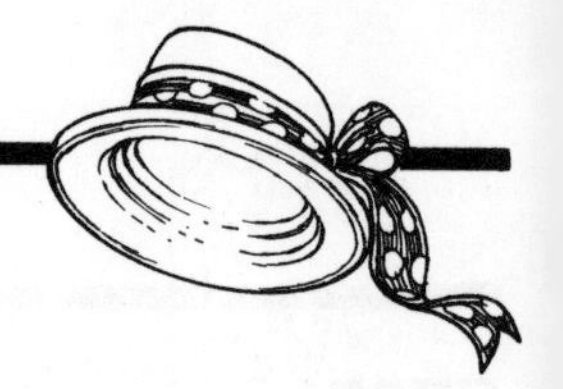

MOVIE NEWS

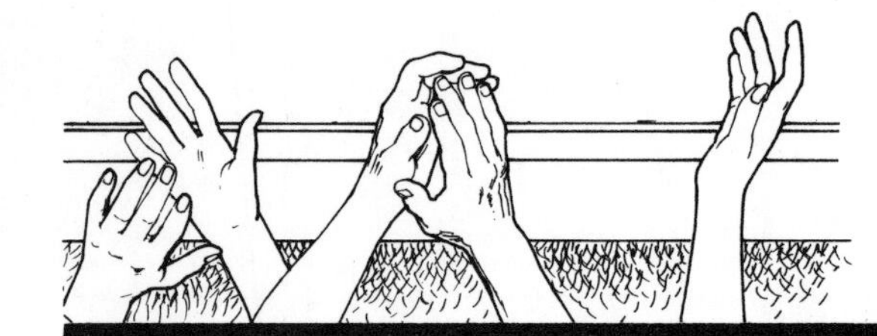

A scene from the best movie of the year

...and a scene from the worst

HORROR MOVIE STARS NEW MONSTER

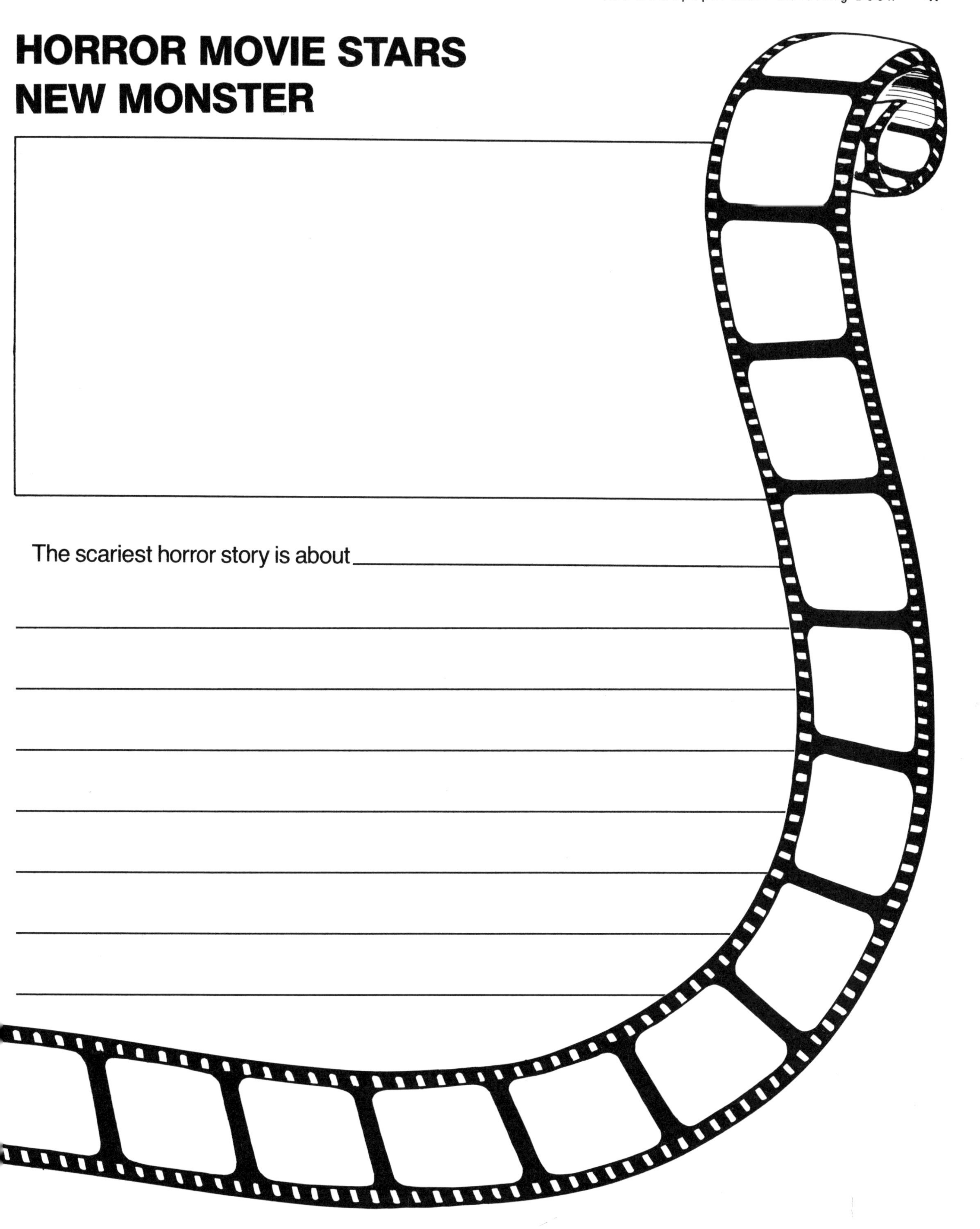

The scariest horror story is about

SCENE FROM HOT NEW MUSIC VIDEO

OUTLINE OF THE NEXT THREE SHOWS FOR FUNNY SITCOM:

1. ______________________________

____

2. ______________________________

____

3. ______________________________

____

SCENE FROM FUNNY NEW SITCOM

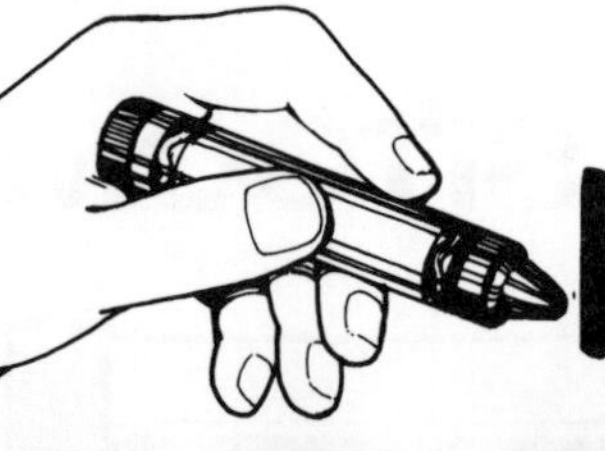

Kids' Pages

By Jo Ann Haun

ACROSS

3 Animal friends
5 Hike and sleep outdoors in a tent
7 A fish's propeller
9 Mix yellow and red to get ___
10 Attach metal to metal with heat
11 Opposite of a lie
12 Stitch
13 Printing machine
16 Newspaper type
17 Not dry
18 No work or school!
20 The science of building
24 Drawing of the surface of an area
27 One of the five continents
29 One who takes care of you in the hospital
30 Picnic invader
31 Related group of people who care for each other
32 Opposite of no
34 Deep red
36 Popular sport
37 Scrambled or fried
40 Pasted picture
42 Sounds of happiness
44 Straight, curvy, or dotted
45 A make-believe face for Halloween
46 Three-dimensional art

DOWN

1 Kind of puzzle
2 Frozen rain
3 Writing tool
4 One of the seasons
5 Modeling material
6 Designed to sell a product
8 Part of the eye
10 Carve wood with a knife
14 Enjoy a book
15 Water sport
16 Art of shaping clay on a wheel
18 Game played with a net
19 Comic strips in a newspaper
21 A Native American people in Arizona
22 Automobile
23 Friends
25 Pretend
26 Dad
28 A cheer
31 Ancient plants and animals preserved in stone
33 Compartments in a barn
35 Compete on a track
38 Mix yellow and blue to get ___
39 Footwear
41 Big bird of Australia
43 The product of creative expression

Answer on page 64

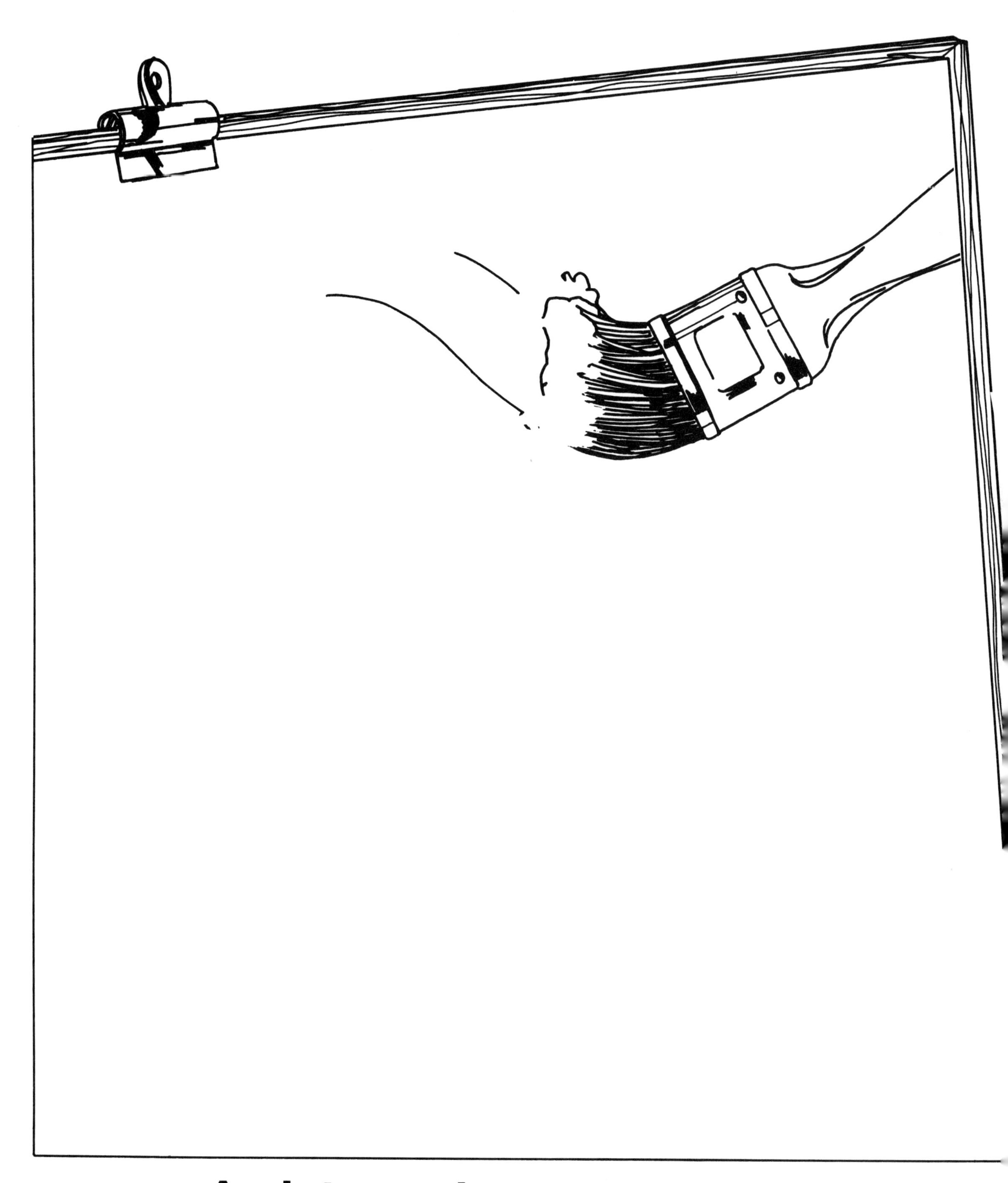

An interesting entry in the city-wide youth art exhibit

COMICS

This comic is designed to make people laugh

This comic pokes fun at society

Child Dreams Up Cartoon Character

A young child had a dream about a new cartoon character. The character is unique and is expected to become as well loved as classics such as Mickey Mouse, Bugs Bunny, or Superman.

The new character is called ______________________

Its special appeal is

______________________ ______________________

______________________ ______________________

______________________ ______________________

Horoscopes

Your star sign is ______________________

What do the stars have in store for you?

____

____

____

____

____

____

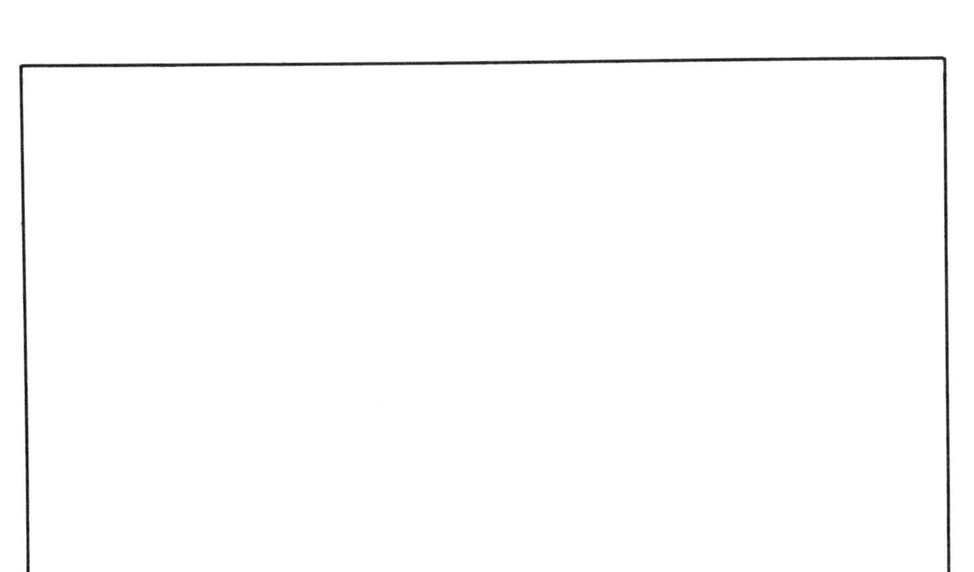

CAPRICORN
Dec. 21–Jan. 19

AQUARIUS
Jan. 20–Feb. 18

PISCES
Feb. 19–Mar. 20

ARIES
Mar. 21–Apr. 20

TAURUS
Apr. 21–May 20

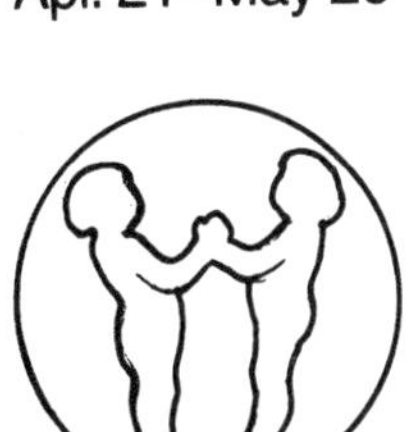

GEMINI
May 21–June 20

CANCER
June 21–July 21

LEO
July 22–Aug. 21

VIRGO
Aug. 22–Sep. 21

LIBRA
Sep. 22–Oct. 21

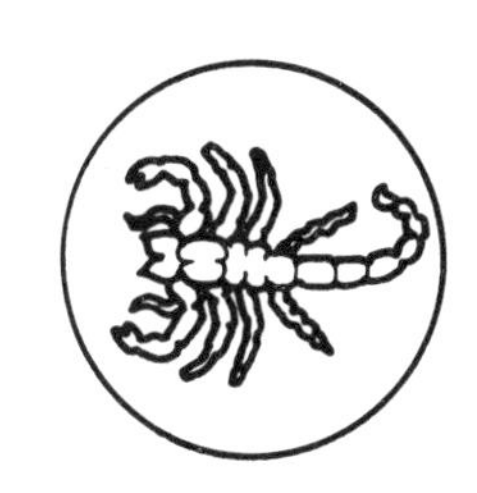

SCORPIO
Oct. 22–Nov. 21

SAGITTARIUS
Nov. 22–Dec. 20

CITY NEWS

THIS ARCHITECT DESIGNED THE LATEST LUXURY APARTMENT BUILDING

A VACANT LOT WAS TURNED INTO A SMALL PARK FOR CITY RESIDENTS

New Skyscraper Erected

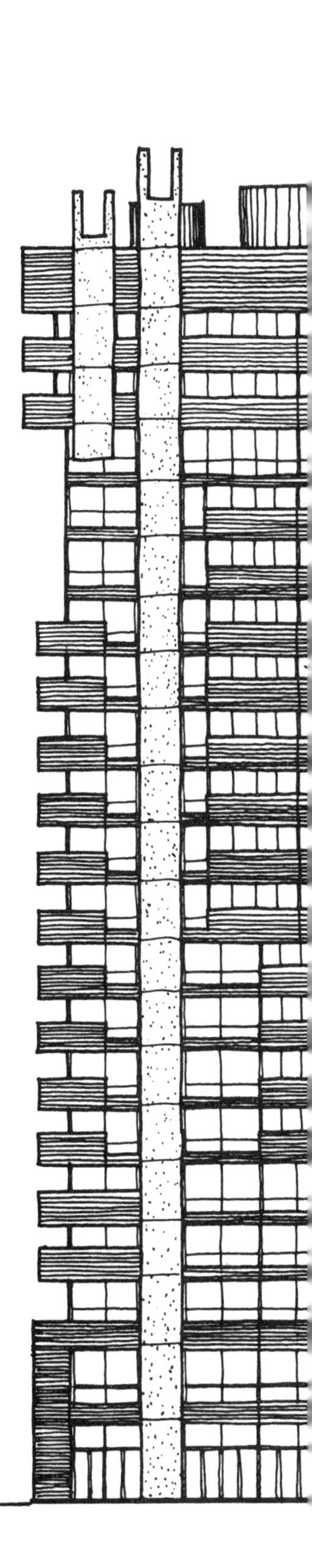

CITY NEWS

City Teen Activities

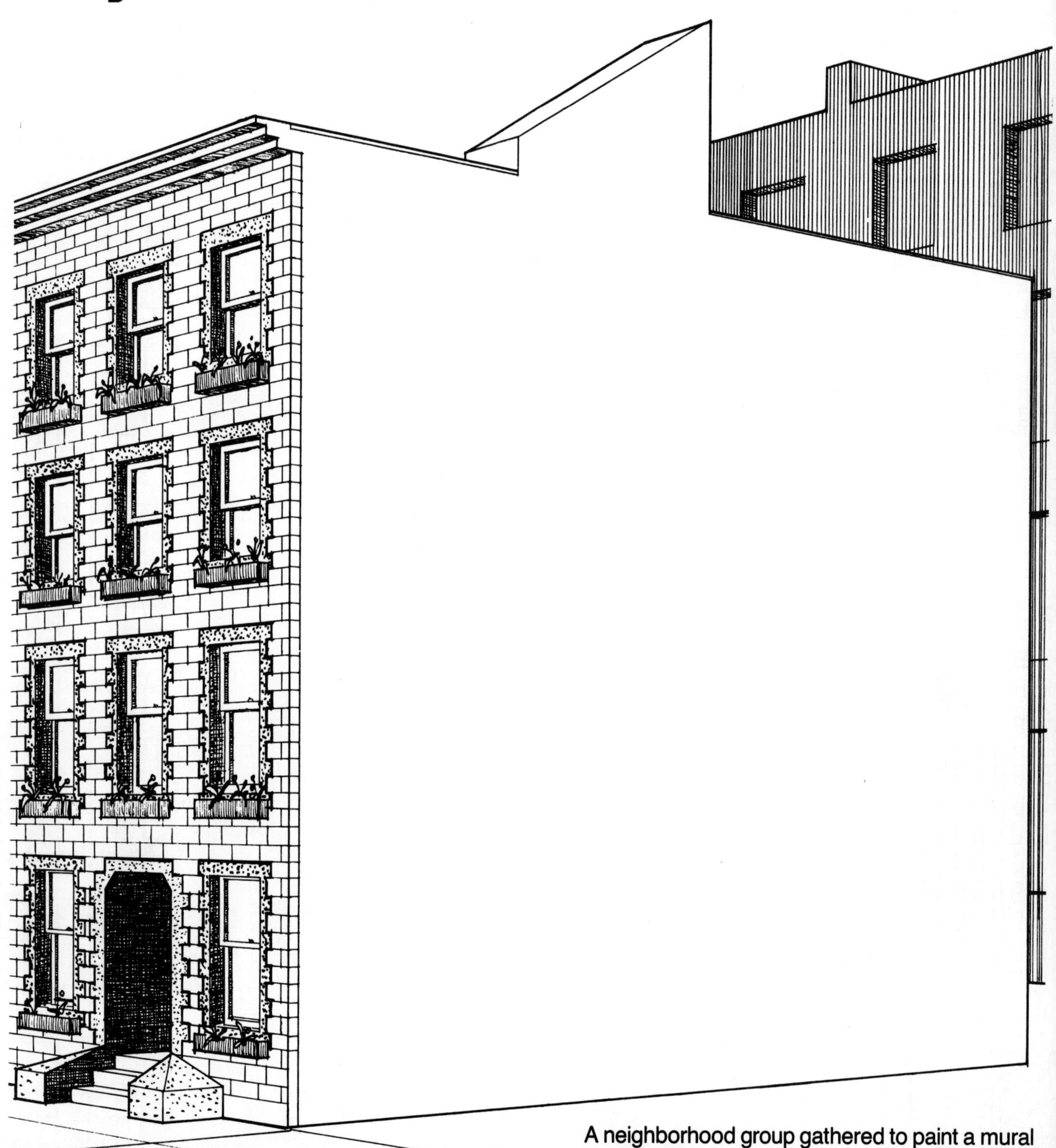

A neighborhood group gathered to paint a mural on the side of this building.

These people are looking with concern at the many changes to life in the country.

House and Garden

Local family tries alternative life-style, creates comfortable home in cave!

Tips on flower arranging given by local florist include these ideas:

Write an ad for and draw a picture of your dream home.

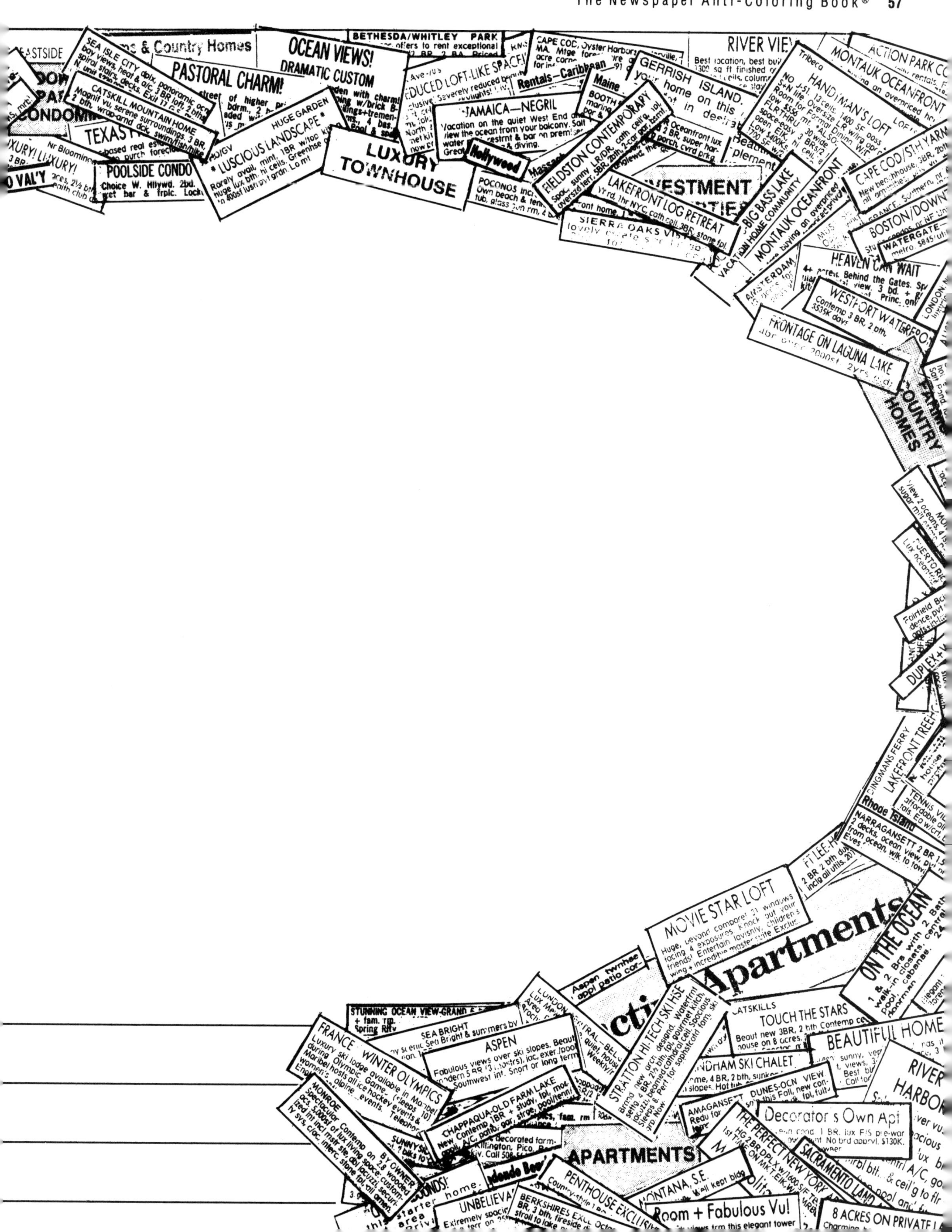

EASTSIDE
BETHESDA/WHITLEY PARK
OCEAN VIEWS!
DRAMATIC CUSTOM
PASTORAL CHARM!
CATSKILL MOUNTAIN HOME
HUGE GARDEN
* LUSCIOUS LANDSCAPE *
POOLSIDE CONDO
LUXURY TOWNHOUSE
JAMAICA—NEGRIL
Rentals—Caribbean
Maine
Hollywood
FIELDSTON CONTEMPORARY
GERRISH ISLAND
RIVER VIEW
HANDYMAN'S LOFT
MONTAUK OCEANFRONT
ACTION PARK
LAKEFRONT LOG RETREAT
SIERRA OAKS
BIG BASS LAKE
VACATION HOME COMMUNITY
CAPE COD/STH YARM
BOSTON/DOWN
WATERGATE
HEAVEN CAN WAIT
WESTPORT WATERFRONT
FRONTAGE ON LAGUNA LAKE
COUNTRY HOMES
DUPLEX
LAKEFRONT TREEHOUSE
Rhode Island
NARRAGANSETT
MOVIE STAR LOFT
Apartments
ON THE OCEAN
TOUCH THE STARS
BEAUTIFUL HOME
RIVER HARBOR
STRATTON HI-TECH SKI HSE
ASPEN
SEA BRIGHT
FRANCE WINTER OLYMPICS
STUNNING OCEAN VIEW
CHAPPAQUA-OLD FARM LAKE
APARTMENTS
Decorator's Own Apt
THE PERFECT NEW YORK
SACRAMENTO LAND
MONTANA, S.E.
PENTHOUSE EXCLUSIVE
BERKSHIRES
UNBELIEVABLE
Room + Fabulous Vu!
8 ACRES ON PRIVATE LAKE
MONROE

Food News

A poll of our readers shows these foods make up their favorite picnic meal.

Cooking School Gives Lesson in Cake Decorating

The head chef at the local cooking school demonstrated the art of cake decorating for our food editors. We learned

Ask a family member for his or her favorite recipe.

From the kitchen of:

Ingredients:

How to prepare:

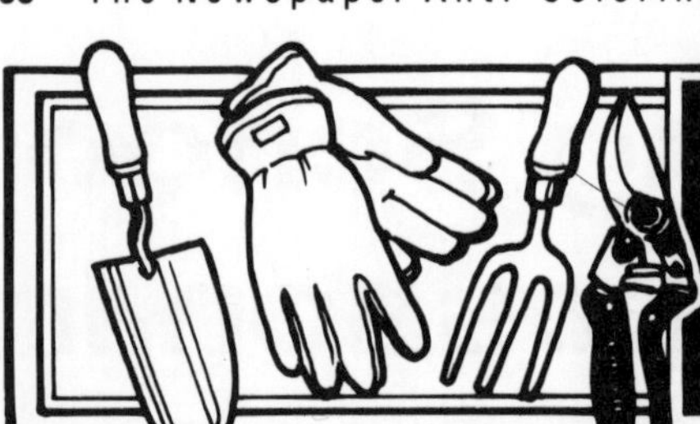

Gardening News

Teens plant community garden

Fanciful water garden created behind lavish new home

You are an important sports figure, shown here playing hard at your favorite sport

Share your secrets for a successful game

Automotive Marketplace

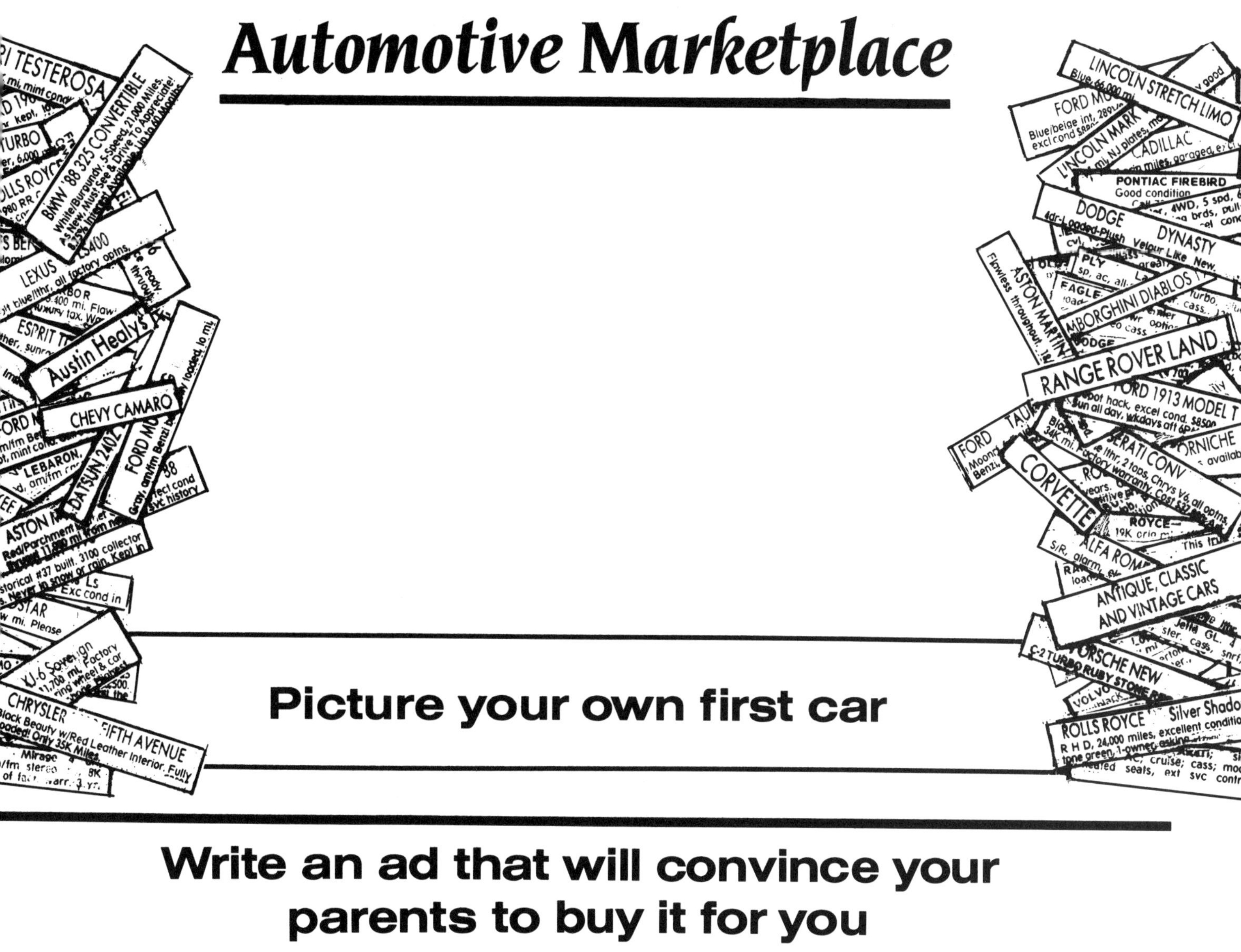

Picture your own first car

Write an ad that will convince your parents to buy it for you

Answer to crossword puzzle

	1 C		2 S		3 P	E	T	4 S					5 C	6 A	M	P		7 F	8 I	N
9 O	R	A	N	G	E			P			10 W	E	L	D					R	
	O		O		N		11 T	R	U	T	H		A						I	
	12 S	E	W					I			I		Y		13 P	14 R	E	15 S	S	
	S				16 P	R	I	N	T		T					E		W		
	17 W	E	T		O			G			T		18 V	A	C	A	T	I	O	N
	O				T				19 F		L		O			D		M		
20 A	R	C	21 H	I	T	E	22 C	T	U	R	E		L		23 P			24 M	25 A	26 P
	D		O		E		A		N				L		27 A	F	28 R	I	C	A
			P		R		R		29 N	U	R	S	E		L		30 A	N	T	
31 F	A	M	I	L	Y				Y				32 Y	E	S			G		
O						33 S			P				B							
34 S	C	A	35 R	L	E	T		36 B	A	S	E	B	A	L	L			37 E	38 G	G
S			A			A			P				L				39 S		R	
I			40 C	O	L	L	A	G	E		41 E		42 L	43 A	U	G	H	T	E	R
44 L	I	N	E			L			R		M			R			O		E	
S				45 M	A	S	K		46 S	C	U	L	P	T	U	R	E		N	